BIRTH
OF THE
FIFTH SUN

BIRTH
OF THE
FIFTH
SUN

AND OTHER
MESOAMERICAN TALES

JO HARPER

Illustrated by
IRMA MARTINEZ SIZER

TEXAS TECH UNIVERSITY PRESS

This book is typeset in Monotype Joanna. The paper used in this book meets the minimum requirements of ANSI/NISO Z39.48–1992 (R1997). ∞

Designed by Lindsay Starr

LIBRARY OF CONGRESS CATALOGING-IN-PUBLICATION DATA
Harper, Jo.
    Birth of the fifth sun : and other Mesoamerican tales / Jo Harper.
        p. cm.
    Summary: "A retelling of traditional folk tales that originate
from Mexico and Central America. They reflect the pre-Colombian,
Mesoamerican worldview, and include characters like Quetzalcoatl
and trickster figures like coyote. A few of the tales are contemporary and seem to originate from Nahuatl-speaking descendants
of the Aztecs"--Provided by publisher.
    Includes bibliographical references.
    ISBN-13: 978-0-89672-625-3 (hardcover : alk. paper)
    ISBN-10: 0-89672-625-8 (hardcover : alk. paper)
1. Indians of Mexico--Folklore. 2. Indians of Central
America--Folklore. 3. Tales--Mexico. 4. Tales--Central America. I.
Title.
    F1219.3.F6H37 2008
    398.2089'97072--dc22   2007045618

Printed in the United States of America
08 09 10 11 12 13 14 15 16 / 9 8 7 6 5 4 3 2 1

Texas Tech University Press
Box 41037, Lubbock, Texas 79409-1037 USA
800.832.4042 | ttup@ttu.edu | www.ttup.ttu.edu

To Lalo

in memory of the good times we've had together

CONTENTS

Acknowledgments   ix
Nahuatl Names and Words   xi

PART ONE Quetzalcoatl and Tezca
Birth of the Fifth Sun   5
Who Will Be the People?   13
Corn Mountain   19
Who Can Teach the People?   23
Music Is Born   27
Quetzalcoatl Falls   35
Tezca Shows His Power   43
Master Log   47
The Pepper Man   53
Tezca's Music   59

PART TWO Tricks and Mistakes
The Thunder Spirits' New Cook   65
The Buzzard Husband   69
Rafael Outsmarts the Nahual   73
Lalito and the Nahual   79
The Devil's Cave   85

The Possum's Tale   89
Chioconejo Rabbit and Coyote   93

Other Tellings   97
Sources   109

Contents

ACKNOWLEDGMENTS

This little book came into being because of my personal friendship with Nahuatl-speaking descendants of the Aztecs. My acquaintance with them began twenty years ago and has broadened and deepened through the years. I cannot recall all the books I have explored or all the conversations I have had about their culture and the shared cultures of Mesoamerica. No doubt I have failed to acknowledge some of my sources of influence. Nevertheless, there are numbers of people to thank. First on the list is Lalo Julian, who gave me stories and encouraged me to write and submit this book. Jorge Julian also took an important interest in it. Frans Schryer, chairman of the department of Sociology and Anthropology at Guelph University, Ontario, read and commented on the manuscript. D. Wayne Gunn, professor emeritus, Texas A&M University–Kingsville, friend, scholar, and faithful reader, has my thanks, as do the wonderful Houston librarians of the University of Houston Library, the Houston Public Library, and the Harris County Library. They were ever ready to help with a search, answer a question, or track down a book.

I am also grateful to the dedicated scholars who preserved the stories; John Bierhorst especially merits heartfelt thanks for his impressive, extensive research. So, although long dead, does the venerable Sahagún on whom we all depend. Thanks also to my daughter Josephine, unparalleled researcher; my daughter De Aaon, meticulous proofreader; and my loyal editor, Judith Keeling.

I have simplified some of the formidable Nahuatl names to make them more accessible. It is my hope that this little volume will add to the appreciation of a much misunderstood and maligned group of people, the Aztecs, and that their many descendants in the United States will enjoy and take pride in this aspect of their heritage.

NAHUATL NAMES AND WORDS

Prior to the Conquest and for some time thereafter, written Nahuatl took the form of pictograms and other symbols. Consequently, Nahuatl words are rendered in slightly different spellings by different scholars.

Nahuatl Names Used in the Text

Cihuacoatl (Snake Woman) See-wah-co-ah-tul
Nanautzin (God who became the Fifth Sun) Na-na-wat-zin
Quetzalcoatl (Peaceful Chief God) Quet-za-co-ah-tul
Tezcatlipoca (War God, enemy of Quetzalcoatl) Tez-caht-lee-po-ka (Tezca, short form)
Tlaloc (Rain God) Tlah-loc

Gods Referred to in English

Lord of the Dead Mictlantecuhtli Mic-tlan-te-coon-tlee
Lord of the Wind Ehecatl Eh-cah-tul
King in "The Pepper Man" Huemac Way-mock
Snake Woman Cihuacoatl See-wah-co-ah-tul

Other

Nahual Nah-wal
Nahuatl Nah-wah-tul
Ahuelican Ah-weh-lee-can

BIRTH
OF THE
FIFTH SUN

Quetzalcoatl and Tezca

BIRTH OF THE FIFTH SUN

The myths of the Aztecs, like the myths of most cultures, attempt to explain the creation of the world, the creation of the people in it, and the development of their culture. The many Aztec gods struggled both with each other and with their own very human failings. Stories about the gods reveal a unique humor that is perhaps one of the most important and unusual aspects of Aztec culture.

The gods decided to make the world, but it was a big job. They hadn't counted on its being so much trouble. They had to dig the ocean and heap up mountains. They had to shape valleys and make lakes and rivers. When all that was done, they had to make a sun. That was the most trouble of all. First they ran up the mountains, down the valleys, and around the lakes collecting light. Then they put together all the light they had caught and shaped it into a great ball. That was their sun. The next thing was to decide who should carry it.

Mighty Tezca, dark and powerful, was very proud of himself. He was fierce and strong as a jaguar. He thought he was the only god glorious enough to carry the sun. He did not consult with the other gods, not even with Quetzalcoatl, the wisest of them all. Instead, Tezca snatched the ball of light, tied it on his back so quickly that nobody could stop him, and leaped into the sky.

The gods were surprised and a little angry, but they said, "Oh, well, Mighty Tezca is quick and strong. Let him carry the sun. We'll call it the Jaguar Sun."

Next the gods made people, but the people they made were large and coarse with big hands, big noses, and big feet. They were giants. They were so big that when they fell, they couldn't get back up again. They had to stay on their feet all the time. It was tiring, but it was necessary. They couldn't bend to scratch their ankles or get thorns out of their feet because if they did they would tip over, and then they were stuck. They had to eat acorns or fruit from high in the trees because they couldn't pick up food from the earth.

Whenever these giants met each other, they would say courteously, "Don't fall!" If they wanted to be very polite, they said it twice. "Oh, don't fall! Don't fall!"

Things were a mess. Because Mighty Tezca was so dark, he cast spots of shadow along with spots of light, and at noon the world went completely dark because he had only enough brightness to last half a day at a time.

Finally, the gods called to Tezca to come down from the sky.

Birth of the Fifth Sun

"Mighty Tezca, you are not a good sun," they shouted. "You are too dark. Your light is too weak."

But Tezca wouldn't come down from the sky. He wouldn't give up his high place. Quetzalcoatl was disgusted. He was so disgusted, he took a big stick and knocked Tezca out of the sky and into the ocean. Tezca was so furious, he changed into a jaguar, leaped from the water, and ate all the giants. That was the end of the first people and the end of the Jaguar Sun.

So all the gods' trouble turned into nothing, and they had to start over. They kept trying to think how to make the sun and how to make people, but they didn't have a good plan. Tezca didn't help at all. He just grouched.

The new people the gods made were a better size than the giants. When they fell over, they could get up, and they were able to pick up food from the ground, but they didn't know about corn.

The gods made one sun that was so weak it blew away in a windstorm, and the people that lived under it were changed into monkeys.

They made another sun that burned itself completely out, and a rain of fire changed the people under that sun into turkeys.

"You gods think you are so smart, but you can't even make a sun. I was a better sun than those," Tezca complained.

At last, it was decided that the Rain God's wife would be a good sun. That was a silly decision, but she became the drippy Fourth Sun. They called her the Water Sun. It rained all the time in the days of the Water Sun, and the people didn't do anything useful at all. They just ate grass and watched the endless rain fall from the sky.

The gods saw that there was going to be a great flood, and they decided to warn one human couple so that they wouldn't have to make people again. They told Tata and Nena that they could save themselves by making a hole in a great tree and hiding in it, but they warned Tata and Nena that they must not be greedy. The gods gave them each one ear of corn. That was all they were supposed to eat. The gods warned them not to touch any other food.

Tata and Nena did make a hole in a great tree. The fierce flood covered the earth, but they stayed in the hole and were safe. They were hungry, though, because the flood lasted a long time.

When the water went down, they climbed out, and as soon as their feet touched the earth, they saw a fish. They remembered that they were ordered not to eat anything besides what the gods had given them, but they were so hungry they caught the fish, built a fire, and cooked it. Smoke from their fire rose into the air and the gods smelled it.

The gods were angry. They complained to each other.

"We saved only one pair of people, and they are disobedient people!"

"We can't put up with people like that."

"Tata and Nena are greedy. They are too greedy to be people."

They told Tata and Nena, "The Water People, your cousins, were as stupid as fish, but still you should not eat them."

Then the gods turned Tata and Nena into dogs.

After a time, the gods gathered together to make another sun. This time they made a great fire and took their places around it. This fire was a mighty fire, a divine fire; it was the creative

fire. And when that fire had burned for four days, the gods said, "The time has come for a new age. Now we must create the Fifth Sun, for the Fourth Sun has run its course like the three suns before it."

The gods decided that to create the Fifth Sun, a strong sun, one of them must throw himself into the fire. But no one moved; no one spoke. None of them wanted to jump into the fire.

At last, someone wrapped in shadows came forward moving slowly, moving timidly. When the light of the divine fire fell on his face, all the gods could see that it was Nanautzin who offered to sacrifice himself.

Nanautzin was small. He was covered with pimples; he was covered with warts and with scabs. He was twisted and ugly, the ugliest of the gods.

When mighty Tezca saw that a twisted ugly god had offered to turn himself into the Fifth Sun, he was angry. The other gods looked at Nanautzin in scorn and muttered to each other that he was not suitable. He was too ugly.

Tezca leaped to his feet and shouted, "Silence! I am strong, handsome, and brave. I will try again. I will be the Fifth Sun!"

The great fire blazed so brightly the stars fled. The sky throbbed, and the sound of drums filled the air. Flames from the divine fire stretched upward, reaching higher and higher.

Then the gods said, "Mighty Tezca, go into the fire."

Tezca smiled a haughty smile, closed his eyes, and took a deep breath. Then he gave a great shout as he ran toward the divine fire. But when he felt the heat of the flames, he lost heart. He could not jump in.

The gods all rose angrily to their feet.

Then, roaring like a hurricane, Tezca once more ran toward the fire. But once more he lost courage.

Four times he ran, and four times his courage failed him. He could not leap into the fire.

Great flames stretched upward. They illuminated the sky. Comets hid in their bright light. The sky beat and throbbed. A hellish howl split the air as the fire itself called to the gods. The howl sounded and resounded through the heavens.

Then the gods, trying not to show their fear, said, "Oh, well, Nanautzin, you might as well try!"

Without waiting, the ugly little god shouted and tore off his clothes. He showed all his ugly body to the creative fire. Then he threw himself in.

Everything went dark. But the gods could hear the crackling of burning flesh.

Suddenly ten thousand rays of light burst in the sky. The heavens opened and took Nanautzin.

Then it was dark again.

The gods sat down, exhausted, to wait for the new sun. They sat and waited. At last a burning red dawn appeared in the east.

A red sun reeled from one side of the heavens to the other.

"The sun isn't following a path through the sky," the gods said. "There cannot be night and day unless the sun is steady." They didn't think about the four bad suns they had made, and they did not appreciate Nanautzin's sacrifice.

Someone called out, "You're not moving right, Nanautzin!"

The sun kept staggering.

Other gods shouted, "Do it right, Nanautzin. Stop staggering!"

"I'm doing the best I can, and you aren't doing anything at all," Nanautzin shouted back. "Stop complaining." And the sun still moved dizzily in the sky.

Then the gods knew that they had to help. Little ugly Nanautzin could not do such a great task alone. They took out their obsidian knives, and screaming, they cut their veins and let out some blood to give the new sun their strength. A great wind carried their blood upward.

The sun steadied in its course. It shone brightly overhead at noon, in the evening it reddened in the west, and the next morning it rose again in the east.

Thus the Fifth Sun, the strongest of the suns, was born. Since that time, it has shone on us all, holding steady in its course.

WHO WILL BE THE PEOPLE?

The gods wanted and needed people. After many failures, they were created through Quetzalcoatl's wit and bravery.

After the birth of the Fifth Sun, the great flood left by the Water Sun dried up. But there weren't any people. Tata and Nena had been turned into dogs, and the other people had either drowned or turned into fishes. The gods kept asking each other, "Who will be the people? Who will be the people?"

The bones of the people of the earlier suns had gone to the Lord of the Dead. Quetzalcoatl knew that the gods could make new people from these bones. At least they were the right size; they just needed to be made smarter. And Quetzalcoatl wanted to make them into smart, strong people who would never die.

Quetzalcoatl decided to go to Mictlan, the Land of the Dead. The journey was long and dreadful even for a god, and it was easy to get lost in the underworld. So Quetzalcoatl gathered some white shells and white pebbles to mark his way, and went down into the earth. The path was rough and crumbling. He struggled downward, and it grew darker with every step. When he dropped a shell or a pebble to mark his way, it was quickly covered with dirt.

The shells and pebbles don't help at all, he thought.

At last Quetzalcoatl came to a river. It was black and wide. He was a strong swimmer, and he was sure he could make it across, but a fierce dog guarded the banks—a dog with rough yellow hair and gleaming amber eyes. The sound of the dog's bark rumbled through the earth like thunder. Boulders and great clumps of dirt fell at the sound. The dog bared his yellow teeth and charged toward Quetzalcoatl as earth crumbled down on him. Quickly, Quetzalcoatl took out a white shell and threw it. The yellow dog turned to look at the gleaming shell.

Quetzalcoatl leaped toward the water. While he was still in the air, the dog jumped back and tore his hand. Quetzalcoatl did not care about the wound. He swam hard and reached the far side of the black river.

At last, he arrived at Mictlan, the dark and gloomy Land of the Dead where skeletons walked and spiders hung in great webs. The Lord of the Dead and his wife were guarding precious bones.

Quetzalcoatl cried, "Give me your bones!"

"Why do you want them?" the Lord of the Dead answered.

"Because we must make people. All the gods keep asking, 'Who will be the people?'"

"Well, you didn't take care of the people you had. Now you have to earn the bones," the Lord of the Dead told Quetzalcoatl.

"You have to show that you really want them and that you deserve them."

"Tell me what I can do," Quetzalcoatl answered, "for we must have people."

"Here, then," said the Lord of the Dead. "Take my trumpet. Blow it and walk four times around my beautiful country. Then you may have some precious bones."

But the Lord of the Dead was sneaky. He gave Quetzalcoatl a trumpet that was not hollow. Even a god could not blow such a trumpet. Quetzalcoatl needed help. What help could he find in the dark, deep Land of the Dead? What living creature was there to help him?

Quetzalcoatl saw that there were worms in the damp earth.

"Help me, worms!" Quetzalcoatl whispered to them. "Hollow this trumpet."

And a mass of worms came crawling. They hollowed the trumpet so air could pass through, and Quetzalcoatl marched around the land blowing the trumpet.

The Lord of the Dead said, "All right. You can have some bones."

Then he spoke to the skeletons. "Quetzalcoatl can't keep the bones forever. Someday he will have to give them back."

The skeletons all shouted at once, "You have to give the bones back!"

The shouting skeletons startled Quetzalcoatl. He answered quickly, before he thought. "No! These bones must live forever."

As soon as Quetzalcoatl said that, he knew he should have lied. The skeletons would try to stop him. Quetzalcoatl was sorry he had spoken. He so was angry with himself, he bit his lip and his tongue.

Then Quetzalcoatl called, "All right. I'll do it. I'll bring them back."

He snatched up the precious bones and began running the long way out of the Land of the Dead and up to the unpeopled earth, but the skeletons knew he had lied. They ran after him screaming, "Give back the bones! Give back the precious bones!"

Quetzalcoatl clutched the bones tightly against his chest and ran hard. He stretched his long legs before him in giant steps. He could hear the bones of the skeletons rattling behind him. But the skeletons had to stay in the Land of the Dead. They could not follow him to the upper earth.

Quetzalcoatl had to cross the wide, black river again. He knew that a little pebble or shell would not delay the dog long enough for him to get away. Even though it made him sad, he knew he must sacrifice one of the precious bones.

He threw one precious bone to the dog and hurried on. When he looked back, the dog was tearing the bone with its great yellow teeth.

By the time Quetzalcoatl reached the upper earth, he was exhausted. He was so tired, he had to rest. He fell into a deep sleep. While he was sleeping, quails sent by the Lord of the Dead swooped down and pecked the bones with their sharp beaks. They broke open the precious bones.

When Quetzalcoatl woke, he got to his feet, looked around him, and saw what had happened. He sobbed aloud and called out, "Oh, how will it be now? How will it be? How will it be?"

Then Quetzalcoatl answered himself. *You know how it will be. The precious bones are broken. Chunks are eaten out of them. Now when you create people they will not live forever. They will die. That's how it will be. The Lord of the Dead will finally have them. You cannot change it.*

Quetzalcoatl could not bear what had happened. He struck himself in the face and covered his face with his hands. He struck himself so hard, the lip he had bitten broke open and began to bleed.

Quetzalcoatl didn't care about his bleeding lip. Still weeping, he gathered up the bones and carried them to the goddess Cihuacoatl, Snake Woman. She ground the bones into meal and put the meal into a jade bowl.

Snake Woman saw that Quetzalcoatl's lip was bleeding. "I will use your blood to make strong people," she told him. "Lean over the bowl and squeeze your lip. Squeeze hard."

He did.

"I need more blood," Snake Woman told him. "Squeeze harder."

Quetzalcoatl didn't care about the pain. He squeezed his lip harder and harder. Then he squeezed the hand that the yellow dog had torn with his great yellow teeth. Blood poured from the wound.

As Quetzalcoatl's blood fell into the bowl, people began to pop out. Men and women sprang from the bowl.

The gods all shouted, "The people have burst forth! They are born of bones and Quetzalcoatl's blood. They will be the people! These are the people!"

CORN MOUNTAIN

The Mesoamerican people had well-developed agriculture. Peppers, squash, beans, and corn were staples of their diet. Corn in particular was the staff of life, their daily bread, and became a symbol of security and plenty.

Being born takes energy. It takes strength. So the new people were very hungry. A lot of corn had been lost in the flood, but not all of it. The gods had put some away because they knew the people had to eat. They kept hoping to create smart people who understood about corn and would soon plant it and grow it for themselves.

When the gods went to get the corn to feed the hungry new people, it was almost all gone. It had been stolen. Only a few scattered grains were left.

"Who has stolen the corn?"

"How will we feed the people?"

"What will the people eat? Will they have to chew grass and leaves? Will they have to peel bark off trees? Oh, what will the people eat?"

While the other gods were wailing and making a fuss, Quetzalcoatl looked around thoughtfully. Almost every living thing had drowned, but Quetzalcoatl noticed something small moving on the ground.

It was an ant hurrying along, carrying a grain of corn.

Quetzalcoatl followed the ant and saw it go into a mountain. He sat and watched. Soon an ant came hurrying out. Before long, it returned with another grain of corn and carried it into the mountain. Other ants did the same.

Now Quetzalcoatl knew what had happened to the corn and where it was hidden. But the mountain was very big, and the holes the ants had made into the mountain were very small. How could Quetzalcoatl get to the corn?

He decided that if he was clever and had enough help, he could manage to get corn for the people. He told the gods to stop making a fuss and go wait quietly by the mountain. Then he went to find the Rain God.

The Rain God was off by himself pouting. He was mad at everyone because his wife, the Water Sun, couldn't be the sun any more. Quetzalcoatl knew the Rain God was in no mood to help, but the people needed corn.

Quetzalcoatl spoke to the Rain God in a friendly way. He praised the way the Rain God darkened the clouds. He admired the way he rolled thunder through the sky. And he exclaimed over the strength of the Rain God's lightning.

"You are the only one who can feed the people," Quetzalcoatl said, "and I'm not sure even you can do it. Do you have the power to open the mountain where the corn is hidden?"

The Rain God's brow darkened. His voice rumbled. He thrust his arm into the air. A great bolt of lightning flashed through the sky. It struck the mountain and split it in two. Corn lay like piles of gold in the opened earth.

The waiting gods rushed into the mountain and began gathering corn for the people. But lightning forked all across the sky. Great claps of thunder shook the trees and even the earth. The Rain God swooped down with his fierce wind and swept most of the corn away. He wasn't satisfied just to split the mountain; he had to take the corn, too. Then everyone depended on him. They could never forget his power.

Sometimes he gave the people plenty of rain and plenty of corn. Sometimes he didn't. And that is the way it still is. That's the Rain God's power.

WHO CAN TEACH THE PEOPLE?

Quetzalcoatl, who was both a man and a god, was known as wise and peace-loving. The only sacrifices he asked for were fruit and flowers. He taught the people many skills. When he was in power, cotton grew high, and the fragrance of flowers filled the air.

It was hard for the people to grow corn. They weren't good at it. As the earth came to have more animals, the people killed them for food and wore their skins for clothes. They did not know how to make cloth. They didn't know how to build houses, either. They wandered from place to place. The gods were getting annoyed. But Quetzalcoatl knew these were not stupid people. They were not lazy people. They could learn if they had someone to teach them. Who could teach the people?

Quetzalcoatl decided that he himself wanted to teach the people, but he knew he would have to have help. He looked around at the gods. All were fierce, jealous, and full of pride, except Snake Woman, who had helped him create the people and who had wanted nothing in return.

Quetzalcoatl found Snake Woman sitting beside her great jade bowl.

"I want to teach the people," Quetzalcoatl told her. "I think I can show them many things, but to teach them, I believe I must become one of them."

Snake Woman nodded agreement.

"Do you know how I could become one of the people?" Quetzalcoatl asked her.

"You must be born," Snake Woman told him. "Find a woman to be your mother."

Quetzalcoatl looked among the people. Some of the women were vain. Some were foolish. Others thought only of themselves and were unkind. Quetzalcoatl searched a long time over many miles. Finally at Tula among the Toltecs, he found a woman named Shemal who stood out from all the rest. He knew Shemal would be a kind, wise mother. When he showed her to Snake Woman, she agreed.

"If we do this thing, you will be a baby. You will have to grow up the way the human people do," she told Quetzalcoatl. "It isn't so easy to grow up. It is trouble."

Quetzalcoatl was in a hurry to teach the people, and he wished Snake Woman would stop talking and get on with it. But she had other things to say. Important things. She told him that he must consider carefully.

"You can teach the people, but whatever you show them, they will learn. They will learn it deeply and forever."

Quetzalcoatl felt strong enough for the task. He was not fierce or prideful or jealous, and he believed he could teach the people good things. He knew he was kind and gentle in his heart. He did not know there was one dark spot in his heart.

"Snake Woman, I will teach the people well," he told her.

Snake Woman reached into her great bowl. She took out a small piece of jade and held it up. The light shone on the jade. It was without flaw.

"Quetzalcoatl, you must be as perfect as this jade."

"I will be perfect," Quetzalcoatl answered.

Then Snake Woman put Quetzalcoatl into the piece of jade and laid it on the path where Shemal was walking.

When Shemal saw the jade, she exclaimed, "How beautiful, so green and smooth!" She picked it up. It was cool, and it shone in her hand.

Shemal felt a terrible hunger. It was a hunger she could not resist. She put the jade in her mouth and swallowed it. She was satisfied.

From the jade, Quetzalcoatl grew in his mother as a baby. When he was born, Shemal took great care of him. She was a strong, wise mother. The little Quetzalcoatl loved her. He was strong and wise, too. He began to teach the people when he was only a child.

MUSIC IS BORN

Tezca was Quetzalcoatl's rival. Unlike Quetzalcoatl, Tezca was selfish and full of pride. He wanted blood sacrifices. He did not care about the people's happiness; he just wanted to be feared and to have power.

In Tula among the Toltecs, Quetzalcoatl grew into a strong wise man. He taught the Toltecs to build houses. He taught the people to make dyes of different colors. They made fine cloth and fine pottery. They learned to raise squash and tomatoes, cacao and cotton, and they grew magnificent corn.

During the years when the infant Quetzalcoatl was growing into a man, Nanautzin, the great and steady Fifth Sun, stayed faithful to his task, but he thought no one appreciated his hard work. Each morning, he rose and lightened the dark sky. Each day he warmed the earth as he made his journey through the heavens. His only company was the Lord of the Wind, who sometimes whistled beside him.

"I like the sound of your whistle," Nanautzin told the Lord of the Wind. "I'm bored when you're not around."

"I know what you mean," the Lord of the Wind answered. "We have lonesome jobs. I whistle to keep up my spirits."

Nanautzin began to sing with the Lord of the Wind. Singing made him happy, but the Lord of the Wind couldn't be with Nanautzin every day. He had to blow rain clouds in from the sea and blow cool air down from the mountains. He had to gust in the spring and storm in the winter.

Nanautzin sang as he walked through the heavens alone, but it wasn't the same. He longed to hear beautiful sounds ringing in harmony. "I need someone to sing with me," Nanautzin told the Lord of the Wind, "but who would walk all the way across the sky every day?"

So the Lord of the Wind found a group of sweet-voiced young spirits and brought them to Nanautzin.

Nanautzin was overjoyed. He wrote songs for the spirits to sing and invented the flute and the drum for them to play. But they still had to be taught, and that wasn't easy. Some of them were lazy and only wanted to rest on fluffy clouds. Some gazed off into the blue and daydreamed. And the youngest, Kiki and Toco, kept running off to romp between sunbeams and slide down rainbows.

Nanautzin worked patiently with the spirits until they became true musicians who loved making music. Even Kiki and Toco would rather play and sing than frolic through the clouds and sunbeams.

The spirits who played and sang cradle songs wore white. Those who sang of love and war wore red. The troubadours of wandering clouds wore blue. And the flute players wore gold that Nanautzin brought from the peaks of the world.

The musicians danced as they played and sang. They kept Nanautzin company on his journey, and they taught new songs to the Lord of the Wind when he came to sing with them.

Since the other gods never visited Nanautzin, they didn't know about his musicians. They hardly noticed his journey through the sky. But one day Tezca was walking through the mountains, and he heard wonderful sounds coming from above. He climbed to the peak of Thunder Mountain, bounding the whole way in his haste to get to the amazing new sounds. From there, he could see the musicians in their colored robes, and he saw that they were making the beautiful melodies.

Tezca wanted the musicians for himself. "I am the Supreme Lord of the World!" he boasted. "Come with me!"

The musicians stopped their circling dance. They did not answer.

"Come!" he shouted again in his dark voice.

The musicians did not move.

Tezca roared. He loosed the thunder from his bottomless throat. He lashed the sky with lightning flashes and whipped flocks of clouds to surround the musicians.

The musicians fled, shrieking melodious notes, dropping their instruments, and tripping on their colored robes. But Tezca snatched them away and took them to his house. Only Kiki and Toco hid from him and escaped.

Day after day, Nanautzin followed his path through the sky,

but he grieved for the musicians who were gone, and he was angry. Even though Kiki and Toco were still with him, and although they played their loveliest tunes, Nanautzin would not be comforted. He began to rise late and set early. At midday, he did not shine brightly. He felt insulted and dishonored. He hid his face.

Things were not so pleasant on earth as they had been before. The corn seeds would not sprout. Without the early sun rays to awaken them, people lay in bed late and neglected their work. Without the bright sun, they did not smile as before.

What is wrong with the Fifth Sun? Quetzalcoatl wondered. Has something happened to Nanautzin? Quetzalcoatl made the long hard climb up Thunder Mountain to find out. "What's the matter, Nanautzin? Are you sick? Why do you rise late and set early? Why don't you shine brightly at noon?"

Nanautzin was so angry he would not answer. He went on his way, pouting. But Kiki and Toco ran to Quetzalcoatl, their colored robes flying behind them. They sang to him, and in their songs, they told him what had happened.

Quetzalcoatl was amazed to hear the songs. "What a marvelous thing music is. The people need music."

Then Nanautzin spoke. "I'm sick and tired of you gods! I do all the work and nobody visits me or gives me any respect. I thought up music. I trained musicians to make my lonely life sweet. But Tezca stole them. Now you want to give away my music. If it weren't for Kiki and Toco, I'd quit shining completely. Then you could make yourself a new sun and start all over."

Quetzalcoatl could see that even though Nanautzin was acting silly, he did have reason to be angry.

"You deserve more honor. That is true," he told Nanautzin. "All the earth and its people depend on you. Keep steady in your course, and I will see what I can do."

Quetzalcoatl went to Tezca's house. He heard beautiful sounds coming from the garden, but the sweet sounds were so mournful, Quetzalcoatl wept to hear them.

"Why are your songs so sad?" he asked.

"Our songs are sad because we are sad."

"We want to dance through the sky with Nanautzin," the blue-robed troubadours told him. They stood quite still, their bodies drooping.

The sunlight gleamed on the flutists' golden instruments. "Perhaps if we stopped playing, if we wouldn't sound even one note, Tezca would send us away, but we love music so much, we must play even though we don't want to be here."

"I think we should fight," a musician in red declared.

Quetzalcoatl held up his hand in a gesture of peace. "Please," he said, "play for me, and lift up your voices." He sat under a tree to listen, and when he heard the songs, he said, "All the world must have music."

He called the Lord of the Wind to come. Then he threw open the garden gate. "Go forth and teach your music," he told the spirits. He did not care what Tezca might say when he returned.

The musicians danced out of the garden playing joyful songs of freedom and triumph. They danced all the way up Thunder Mountain to the top of the world. As they danced and played and sang, the Lord of the Wind seized their joyful sounds and tossed them into the air before him. He whistled the music down into the valleys and forests. He spread the songs over the plains and seas. The branches of the trees lifted as the voices of the people awakened. The wings of the quetzal birds fluttered. The faces of flowers turned toward the songs, and the cheeks of the fruit glowed as music spread to the four quarters of the earth.

Quetzalcoatl thought about Nanautzin, faithfully following his course in the heavens. He thought about what a wonderful thing the creation of music was, and he knew that Nanautzin deserved honor.

So Quetzalcoatl made a plan. He needed to tell Nanautzin, but he didn't want to climb all the way up Thunder Mountain again, so he asked the Lord of the Wind to carry a message:

Honored Fifth Sun, Great Nanautzin—Each morning at dawn, Quetzalcoatl and his followers will go down to the water and pierce their ear lobes with thorns. They will toss drops of blood to you as you rise. This will nourish you. Each morning they will blow a trumpet in your honor and sing a song of praise to you, the Giver of Life, the Giver of Music.

And thus it is. Every morning the earth sings to the sun, and Nanautzin and his musicians sing back. All the earth and sky sing at dawn.

QUETZALCOATL FALLS

The great and good Quetzalcoatl, who wanted only fruit and flowers in sacrifice and who worked so endlessly for his people, was not perfect. He had one dark spot in his heart, and it brought him low, tricked by Tezca.

Quetzalcoatl loved the Toltecs and they loved him. He wanted to be near them, and they wanted to be near him, so with his helpers, he built four houses among them. They built a turquoise house, a house of coral, a house of white shell, and a house of precious blue-green quetzal plumes. They furnished each with rugs woven of flowers, wall hangings woven of feathers, and lovely multicolored mosaics. Fountains splashed in the fragrant gardens.

Wherever Quetzalcoatl went, singing birds went with him. The breeze whispered gently around him, and the air was filled with perfume. Each morning at dawn, he and his helpers went down to the water and performed the rites he had promised Nanautzin. They pierced their ear lobes with thorns. They tossed drops of blood to the rising sun to show respect and to nourish it. The only offerings Quetzalcoatl wanted for himself were fruits and flowers.

Tezca was jealous because the people loved Quetzalcoatl. His fierce face grew stormy as he thought about it. "I'm better than Quetzalcoatl. The Toltecs should follow me. I want them to fight wars. I want human sacrifices."

He brooded a long time, and he made himself a dreadful promise. "I will drive such a wedge between Quetzalcoatl and his people that he can no longer walk among them. I will tear him from the heart of the Toltecs. I will drive him out."

Tezca got the clearest, purest water. He got the finest sand. He got strong metal. And from Tlaloc he got bolts of lightning. Then he went to work deep in the mountain where no one could see. His muscles bulged and sweat dripped from his brow as he forged a magic mirror. When it was finished, he wrapped the mirror in linen and took the form of a stooped, white-haired old man. He carried the mirror to the coral house where Quetzalcoatl was staying.

"Tell Quetzalcoatl I have come to show him his flesh," he told the helper at the door of the coral house.

When the helper told Quetzalcoatl of the visitor, he said, "What does he mean, my flesh? Look and see what he has brought."

But the old man wouldn't show it to anyone but Quetzalcoatl. So Quetzalcoatl said, "Let him come in."

Tezca entered, and Quetzalcoatl spoke politely. "You have tired yourself, Grandfather. Where do you come from?"

Tezca answered, "Quetzalcoatl, I've come to show you your flesh."

"What is this 'flesh' of mine? Let me see it."

Then Tezca gave Quetzalcoatl the mirror, and said, "See yourself. Know yourself. Look in the mirror."

Quetzalcoatl was a tall, large-bodied man, broad-browed and great-eyed, with long black hair and a heavy beard. He was a fine-looking man. But when Quetzalcoatl looked in the mirror, he saw something very different from his real self. He was horrified to see a man whose eyelids bulged, whose eye sockets were sunk deep, and whose face was lumpy all over. He was monstrous.

Mild, gentle Quetzalcoatl did not know that the mirror lied. "Oh, I am horrible, too horrible to be seen," he said. "My people must never look at me."

Tezca smiled a secret, wicked smile and went away. Quetzalcoatl stayed deeply hidden in the back of his coral house.

But Quetzalcoatl grew lonely for his people. He longed to be with them, so he made himself a magnificent head fan of feathers and made a turquoise mask with serpent teeth. He was pleased with his costume. No one would be offended by what he thought was his ugly face.

Quetzalcoatl went out from the coral house and walked among the people again. They were glad to see him even though his head was covered with feathers and he wore a mask with serpent teeth. They walked with him between the fields of corn and among the fruit trees. Together they made offerings of bread, roses, perfumes, and incense.

Tezca was angry because Quetzalcoatl had come out of hiding and was walking among his people. So he thought of another cruel plan. He gathered together greens, tomatoes, chilies, corn, beans, and magueys. He made the magueys into pulque and mixed it with tree honey. Then, again as an old man, he went to Quetzalcoatl's coral house. He told the helpers to tell Quetzalcoatl that someone was there to see him who had come a long way.

Quetzalcoatl said, "Let him come in."

First Tezca presented the fresh, tender vegetables. When Quetzalcoatl had eaten, Tezca offered him pulque, but Quetzalcoatl hesitated. It smelled odd.

Tezca said, "This is a good drink. It will make you feel happy. Taste it with your finger."

Quetzalcoatl tasted a drop from the tip of his finger. It seemed good. It seemed wholesome. So he said, "Let me drink, Grandfather."

Tezca gave Quetzalcoatl a glass of pulque. He gave a glass to each of his helpers, also. The pulque tasted wonderful. Quetzalcoatl emptied his glass quickly. He did not notice that it was making him drunk. He only noticed that it tasted good and that he was very thirsty.

Tezca gave him a second glass, and he gave a second glass to all his helpers.

Again Quetzalcoatl drank quickly. The drink made him happy.

Tezca filled the glasses a third time. Quetzalcoatl and his helpers joked and laughed. Tezca filled the glasses a fourth time. Quetzalcoatl and his helpers boasted to each other. They began dancing. They clapped their hands and threw their feet high. They did not know how foolish they looked.

Tezca filled the glasses a fifth time. Quetzalcoatl and his helpers fell when they tried to dance. Tezca smiled.

Quetzalcoatl's mother, Shemal, felt uneasy and came to visit him. When she saw him, she exclaimed, "My beloved son, look what you are doing. You, the highest teacher, are brought low. Oh, Quetzalcoatl, what are you teaching the people?"

Quetzalcoatl flew into a rage. He struck his mother and shouted, "Don't talk to me like that, old woman. You are mortal and will die. I will live forever!"

Shemal went sadly home.

Now Tezca knew that his evil plan had worked. He smiled his wicked smile and said, "Sing, Quetzalcoatl. Here's a song for you:

> I must leave my house of quetzal,
> my house of turquoise,
> my house of coral,
> I must leave my house of white shell.

At dawn Quetzalcoatl and his helpers did not go down to the water to pray and nourish the sun. They lay drunk. Without nourishment, Nanautzin, the Fifth Sun, moved uncertainly in the sky.

When Quetzalcoatl and his helpers came to themselves, they realized that they had neglected their duties and hurried to perform them. They were ashamed and filled with sadness.

Quetzalcoatl wept. He went to beg Shemal's forgiveness. Then his mother sang a lament about how he would have to go away.

You must leave your house of quetzal,
your house of turquoise,
your house of coral,
You must leave your house of white shell.

Shemal understood as Quetzalcoatl's helpers did not, that he had done a most dreadful thing. She grieved with him. Together Quetzalcoatl and his mother thought about the words of Snake Woman, "*Whatever you teach them, they will learn. They will learn it deeply and forever.*"

Quetzalcoatl and Shemal knew he had taught the people drunkenness, disrespect, and violence. They grieved because of the sorrow that would come.

Quetzalcoatl embraced Shemal and left. His helpers followed him singing,

Once Quetzalcoatl shone like perfect jade.
Now the jade is broken.
Let us weep for the broken jade.

No one knows what happened next. Some people say that Quetzalcoatl and his helpers reached the ocean at the darkest hour before dawn and built a great fire and that Quetzalcoatl made a low bow and leaped into it. A quetzal rose from the fire, and the morning star appeared in the sky.

Other people say Quetzalcoatl sailed out to sea on a raft of snakes, and that someday he will return. Those people watch and wait for him.

TEZCA SHOWS HIS POWER

Now that Quetzalcoatl is gone, Tezca thought, the Toltecs will be my people. They will follow my command. They will offer sacrifices to me and be loyal to me.

But the people did not follow Tezca's fierce, bloody ways. They remembered Quetzalcoatl's gentleness and wisdom. They kept him in their hearts.

Tezca became angry. Each day when he saw the people make offerings of fruit and flowers, he scowled. He decided to show the people his power. He thought that when they saw how mighty he was, they would be overcome with wonder and would follow him.

He chose a beautiful day to present himself to the people. They were in the garden at Tula, enjoying the fresh breeze and fragrant flowers. Suddenly Tezca appeared among them, shining and magnificent. He stood larger than any of the people, and he carried a thunderbolt as a staff. His skin glistened, and his great brow furrowed. His mighty voice boomed, "Toltecs, look at me!"

The Toltecs were not struck with wonder and amazement as Tezca had intended. They were struck with fear and horror. Instead of bowing, they turned and ran away.

Tezca was enraged. He pointed his staff at the people. Thunder clapped, and jagged streaks of lightning burst from his staff. Toltecs dropped like fallen blossoms. The dead lay among the flowers.

Tezca did not mourn. He did not care about the fallen Toltecs. He turned his back and left the garden, taking long strides.

But he was still determined that he would be the preferred god, the lord of the Toltecs. And he still thought that when they understood his power, they would fall down and worship him.

The very next day, he walked through the streets of Tula, his head high and his eyes glittering, but the people did not bow down and honor him. They turned their heads. They hurried out of his path.

Tezca was furious. "Watch, Toltecs!" he thundered. He raised his hand, and a great rock fell in front of him. It seemed to come from nowhere.

"I am the strongest of all! Worship me! Make blood sacrifices!"

But the Toltecs hurried away to hide in their houses.

Tezca lifted his angry hand again and again. A torrent of stones fell from the sky. Falling stones bruised the Toltecs. Great

rocks knocked them off their feet. Boulders crushed them in their paths.

Tezca did not care about the Toltecs' pain. He did not sorrow for their deaths. He turned his back and took long strides out of the city. He went into the mountains and sat sulking in a dark cave. He did not want to see Nanautzin's cheerful rays. He did not want to look at the blue sky or hear the music of the brook.

MASTER LOG

Even with Quetzalcoatl gone, the people remember him and his peaceful ways. Tezca vows to take revenge on them because they will not worship him. He conceives of a bizarre way to take revenge. This story is an excellent example of the way the Aztecs combined humor with horror.

Tezca sat in the gloomy cave. His black heart twisted with rage. "I have shown the people my power, but they still do not worship me," he said to himself. "The Toltecs are stupid, wicked people. Quetzalcoatl thinks he taught them to be good and wise, but he is wrong, and I will prove it. Then I will take my revenge."

Tezca came out of the darkness of the cave and went into the city of Tula, fragrant with perfumes of flowers. But he did not go in his ordinary tall and powerful form. He went disguised as a traveling entertainer and sat in the park in the center of town.

"My name is Master Log," he announced, "and this is Blue Hummingbird."

He stretched out his hand. In it appeared a tiny man dressed in bright feathers. The little man danced on his palm. The air above him shimmered as he moved. Those who saw Blue Hummingbird could not look away.

People were amazed at the sight of the dancing man, no bigger than a hummingbird. They crowded close to Master Log. More and more people came running to see Blue Hummingbird. The excited people pushed and shoved. Some of them stumbled and fell. The Toltecs did not help their friends who had fallen. Instead, they kept their eyes on Blue Hummingbird and trampled those who had fallen under foot. Forty Toltecs were killed.

Master Log closed his hand, and Blue Hummingbird disappeared. Master Log turned and left.

The next day, Tezca returned as Master Log. "I am here. Come see Blue Hummingbird."

Toltecs came running. Caught in Tezca's spell, they longed to see the bright little dancer. They were even more excited than the day before.

Tezca stretched out his hand. Blue Hummingbird danced. His colors shimmered. Again Toltecs crowded around Master Log. Again they pushed and shoved. Again some fell and other Toltecs trampled them. A few of the Toltecs realized what they were doing, but they kept pushing forward, weeping as they stepped on their brothers. When forty had died, Master Log closed his hand, and Blue Hummingbird disappeared. Master Log turned and left.

The same thing happened on the third day and on the fourth day, but on the fourth day, Master Log did not leave. He addressed the Toltecs. "Why do you let me do this to you? Why don't you kill me?"

Still under his spell, the people gathered stones and hurled them at Master Log. The Toltecs killed Master Log, just as Tezca had wanted them to. He thought this proved that the people Quetzalcoatl loved were unworthy people.

Then the second part of Tezca's plan began. The corpse of Master Log began to stink. The poisonous stench was terrible.

"We must take Master Log out of the city," one man said. He tried to move the body, but it would not budge. Strong men gathered around and tried to move the corpse, but they could not. They tied ropes around the body so many men could heave all together. Still Master Log could not be budged. The foul odor choked the workers. They felt sick and dizzy. At last, exhausted, the men went home to rest.

All over Tula, even to the house and gardens of the king, the Toltecs could not breathe. Strong people gasped. Infants cried fretfully. The aged and infirm moaned softly. That night, many Toltecs died from the terrible stench that choked the once-fragrant city of Tula, the city once sweet with the scents of night-blooming flowers.

The sun rose on deserted streets. No one worked. No one played. The strongest men of Tula went to where the corpse of Master Log lay. Gasping, they caught hold of the ropes and all heaved together. But Master Log seemed to be fastened to the earth.

Tezca was bored. He had intended to lie firm. His plan was

to remain as the rotting corpse of Master Log until all the people of Tula died a gruesome death. He thought that Quetzalcoatl's followers deserved gruesome deaths, but he hated lying still.

Master Log was heavier than all the stones the people of Tula had cast at him. This time as the men heaved, Master Log moved. He began to roll, and he rolled over the strong men. Before they could leap out of the way, Master Log crushed them under his great weight.

Thus were many Toltecs slain.

THE PEPPER MAN

Tezca continues his search for revenge. Even the king and the king's daughter do not escape his trickery. He wants to punish all the Toltecs because they do not love and worship him.

Many Toltecs had been slain, but many still lived. Tezca's revenge was not complete. He returned to the dark mountain cave to make another plan. He thought a long time. At last, he was ready.

Because Quetzalcoatl had chosen Atmoc as king for the Toltecs, Tezca vowed to bring him down. He would destroy King Atmoc and all his people. Tezca vowed to take revenge on all the followers of Quetzalcoatl, the high and the low, all those who paid tribute with fruit and flowers.

Tezca assumed the guise of a poor young foreigner, a vendor of chili peppers, and went into the marketplace in Tula.

The young foreigner was very handsome. He drew people's eyes. When Lali, the daughter of the Toltec king, went to the market and saw the young stranger, she could not take her eyes off him. She wanted to look at him and be near him. At home, she thought of him all day and dreamed of him at night. She wanted to spend all her time at the market so she could gaze on him.

All Lali's friends and attendants told her that the young foreigner was only a poor man, a lowly pepper salesman. He was not suitable for her. She knew that her father would say the same. At last, Lali fell sick. She could not sleep. She could not eat. She barely had the strength to go to the market in the afternoon to gaze on the young stranger, who seemed not to notice her at all. Finally, Lali could not rise from her bed.

Lali's father loved her dearly. When he learned how sick his daughter was, he sent for Old Cheema, the wisest woman in Tula to nurse her and look for a cure. When Old Cheema had been with his daughter for two days, King Atmoc sent for her.

"What is it that ails my daughter?" he asked.

"It's love sickness," Old Cheema answered. "Love is a killer."

"Who does my daughter love, and why has love made her sick? It is true that she is young. I would rather she married late. Still, she can have any man she wishes, even the richest man in Tula. Lali should know this."

"She knows it."

"Then, Grandmother, why does she waste away?"

Old Cheema explained that Lali had fallen in love, not with one of the greatest men in Tula, but with a poor pepper vendor,

a foreigner. Lali knew this was unsuitable, and she had resolved to starve herself.

King Atmoc rose. "Unsuitable or not, my daughter shall have who she wishes."

He sent for the pepper vendor, who came into his presence dressed in rags.

King Atmoc groaned. Then he asked, "What have you done to my daughter? Have you enchanted her?"

"No, King," Tezca lied. "I don't know your daughter. I am just a pepper man." He spoke with a strange accent.

King Atmoc groaned again. Then he said, "My daughter is sick for love of you. She shall have you if she wishes, for she must be cured."

King Atmoc sent the pepper man to be washed and dressed in fine clothes. Then he had Lali brought into his presence. She cried out in surprise and joy when she saw the pepper man, and her father commanded that a wedding take place at once. This cured Lali, but it made the people angry. They did not want a strange foreigner to be in their royal family. A stranger, not of their own people, should not be so close to the Toltec throne.

Tezca chuckled in his wicked heart. He had united with the highest of the Toltecs. Now they must bow to him. But Tezca was not satisfied with his place of honor or with his beautiful young wife who loved him. He hungered for revenge, and his thoughts were dark, dark thoughts. *I will make Quetzalcoatl's peaceful people turn to war. I will turn them into killers, and I will be honored for it.*

Tezca disguised himself and went into the streets. He spoke vile words about the new prince. He sowed the seeds of discontent. He planted hatred. He cultivated anger. At last, the people boiled with rage. They rose up and rebelled against their king. People who had once followed the peaceful ways of Quetzalcoatl now armed themselves and made war.

Pretending to be the King Atmoc's defender, Tezca went out with an army. It was a weak army made up only of the king's old friends—old men, many of them lame. This did not matter to Tezca. It suited his plan, for he was matchless in war.

Tezca led the weak army of old and crippled men to a great victory. In doing so, he brought many brave young Toltecs to their deaths, but he was honored as a faithful defender of the king. To celebrate the victory, Tezca invited all the people of Tula to a great festival from sunset until midnight.

Tezca led the dancers round and round. He sang jubilant songs. The dance grew wilder and wilder.

"Follow me!" Tezca called out. "Follow me!" His young wife danced behind him. King Atmoc danced after her. And all the people followed them.

Tezca led them onto a bridge above a deep river. As they were massed there, dancing wildly, Tezca caused the bridge to fall. He himself leaped off just before it fell.

Thus Tezca destroyed the Toltecs.

TEZCA'S MUSIC

Tezca is not completely evil. He finds that he has a white spot in his dark heart. He plays the flute and becomes a pied piper.

Tezca had destroyed the Toltec people. No one remained except young children who had not attended the dance and the women who cared for them. Only these. Yet Tezca felt that his work was not done.

He did not go to the dark cave to ponder. Instead, he went to his house and sat in his garden. A light breeze rustled in the trees and a fountain burbled. Tezca took out the flute he had learned to play when the musicians were with him. He played one tune after another, sweet sounds, mellow sounds, happy and sad sounds, slow sounds, and quick sounds.

After Tezca had played for a long time, he returned to the empty streets of Tula. The only sounds in the city were the soft sobs of Toltec children and the grieved wails of their caretakers. For the first time, Tezca felt a pang of pity. He had not known that there was a white spot deep in his dark heart.

He began to lightly play his flute. He blew a quick, lilting melody, a tune like musical laughter. Tezca did not hurry in his playing. He simply sat in the town square and made music. Slowly there began to be movement in the courtyard. Tezca did not look up. He kept playing. Soon there were soft steps near him. Something touched his knee. Tezca moved gently so as not to startle the children he knew were surrounding him. They were gathered in little clusters on the square, their caretakers beside them.

Tezca smiled. He began to play another tune. It was a tune to set feet dancing. Then Tezca rose and started out of Tula, still playing. All the children and their caretakers followed him. Away they danced, across the plains, up the hills, down the valleys, and all across Mexico.

These are my followers, Tezca thought. They will people Mexico. They will be great warriors. They will offer sacrifices to me. They will honor me all their days.

When they reached the place of the seven caves, Tezca stopped playing and returned home. His work was done. He thought he had destroyed all of the followers of Quetzalcoatl. He thought he was now the god most honored by all the people. But Tezca had not won completely. Some children remembered the teachings of their parents. Some caretakers kept to their old beliefs. They kept the gentle ways of Quetzalcoatl. They offered fruit and flowers as offerings. They knew Quetzalcoatl would return on his raft of snakes and teach them again.

To this day, they wait for his return.

Tricks and Mistakes

THE THUNDER SPIRITS' NEW COOK

This is a humorous story of god-human interaction.
Tlaloc's helpers, who are lesser gods, choose a helper
carelessly. The helper is hopelessly inept and causes
them trouble.

One day a man named Keely was walking down the road.
He was just walking along, minding his own business,
when he saw some Thunder Spirits. These Thunder Spirits
were the helpers of the Rain God, Tlaloc. The Thunder Spirits
snatched Keely up and whisked him away with them. They
needed someone to cook and help around the house, so they
took him to the Rain God's home in the sky.

The Thunder Spirits showed Keely the Rain God's house. It
had four big rooms on the four sides of a big courtyard. In each
room, there was a big water pot. Each pot contained rain. All

the rains of the world—warm, cold, gentle, and fierce—were gathered there for the Rain God's use.

The Thunder Spirits gave Keely some of the wholesome water. They measured out some beans and told him to cook them. Then they left the house wearing rain capes and carrying swords. They ran, their capes making crackling sounds and their swords flashing as they made rain.

Keely boiled the water so he could cook the beans. He did that right, but when he put in the beans, he thought, "*Ha! These beans are not enough. Better throw in a few more.*"

He went where food was stored, got more beans, and tossed them in the pot. When they began to cook, they swelled up and kept swelling. They boiled out of the pot and spread all over the floor. Keely tried to clean them up but they just kept boiling onto the floor.

The Thunder Spirits came home, took off their capes, piled them in a corner of the courtyard, and laid their swords beside them. Then they went into the house for their supper of freshly cooked beans, and they found a big mess.

"You put in more beans!" the Thunder Spirits complained.

They were mad at Keely. They grumbled in their rumbly voices, but they sat down and ate.

While they were eating and not paying attention, Keely slipped into the courtyard. He put on one of the Thunder Spirits' capes and picked up one of their glittering swords. He went running out wearing the cape and waving the sword. It began to rain.

Keely felt powerful. He ran and ran. He shook the cape and flashed the sword as he went.

Rain poured. It fell in great sheets. It was a deluge. Below, water rose in the maize fields, and people worried that the corn would wash away. They worried that they might drown.

The Thunder Spirits looked among themselves and saw that not one of them was missing. No Thunder Spirit was causing the flood. They looked through the dark clouds to see what was causing the terrible rain, and they found Keely. He was running, the cape streaming behind him and the sword flashing in front of him.

The Thunder Spirits dashed after Keely and caught him. They took away the cape and the sword. "You can't be our cook," they told him. "You are too much trouble. You had better go back where you came from!"

The next thing Keely knew, he was walking along the road just as he had been before the Thunder Spirits carried him away, except now he was walking in deep mud.

THE BUZZARD HUSBAND

Is it better to be a man or a buzzard? Chiwa thought the buzzard had all the advantages. Later he has reason to change his mind, but it is too late to change his fate.

Once there was a very lazy man named Chiwa. He didn't want to work in the corn fields. He didn't want to bring in firewood. He didn't want to do any work around his house. He didn't want to do anything to support his wife and children. He just wanted to loaf all day.

His wife and children and even the neighbors complained, but it didn't do a bit of good.

One morning Chiwa strolled away from his house. Soon, he felt tired and sat on a stone. He saw a buzzard circling overhead. He spoke out loud to himself and said, "Just look at that lucky buzzard. He doesn't do any work, and no one complains. No one even cares. He is as free as can be. I would like to have that kind of life."

The buzzard swooped near, and Chiwa called, "Come down here, Buzzard. I want to talk to you."

The buzzard came down and perched near Chiwa.

"I want to be a buzzard. I like your kind of life," Chiwa told the buzzard. "All you do is fly through the air, and no one bothers you about doing work. I am tired of working. I don't want to work any more."

"You can change if you want to," the buzzard told him, but then you can't eat tortillas. You have to eat dead horses, dead cows, dead chickens, and dead pigs. Buzzards only eat dead things."

"Oh, that's no problem," Chiwa said. "I can eat anything."

"Well, then, I'll switch with you," the buzzard said. "I'd rather be a man than a buzzard. Just jump in the air three times."

Chiwa wasn't too lazy for that. He really wanted to be a buzzard. So he leaped high. He made the best jumps he could, one, two, three.

After the third jump, Chiwa turned into a buzzard, and the buzzard turned into a man.

Chiwa was happy. *Now I have found the good life,* he thought.

He flew all around. He flew high over hills and low in valleys. He flew over villages and farms. When he flew over his own house, he saw his wife and children below, and he smelled the corn his wife was cooking. It smelled so sweet, he wanted to eat it with his family. He was ready to go home. The buzzard who had become a man was below, too.

I can't really eat buzzard food, Chiwa thought.

He flew to the ground. He jumped one, two, three, but he was still a buzzard. He tried again and again, but he couldn't jump back into being a man.

While he was jumping, the buzzard-turned-man went into the house. The woman said, "What have you been doing? You stink something awful. Get away from me. You aren't like you used to be."

"What are you talking about?" the buzzard-turned-man said to the woman. "I have always smelled like this."

Just then a buzzard flew into the house. It flew all around and wouldn't leave. The woman got a stick and began to hit it, but the buzzard wouldn't go away.

"Horrible buzzard! Horrible, horrible buzzard!" she shouted. She struck it again and again. But still the buzzard did not go away.

"What is going on? A buzzard has never come into our house before," the woman said to the buzzard-turned-man. "Are you too lazy to get that buzzard out of the house?"

Then the buzzard-turned-man told the woman the truth.

She began to cry, but that didn't change anything. Her husband couldn't become a man again. He would be a buzzard for the rest of his days and eat the food that buzzards eat. But it didn't turn out so badly for the woman after all. She made the buzzard-turned-man take several hot baths, one after the other, and he proved to be a better worker than her first husband.

RAFAEL OUTSMARTS THE NAHUAL

The Aztec people are troubled by *nahuals*. A nahual is a person who is also an evil spirit. At night this spirit can change from human to animal by turning flips, but when morning comes, he will turn back into a person whether he wants to or not. Nahuals can make people see visions. A person might be on a farm, but the nahual can make him think he is in a canyon or on a battle-field. A nahual does not touch his victims. He injures them with his spirit, but to actually kill them he needs to find them asleep. When a nahual kills a person, the Aztecs say he eats the person's heart.

Canciano lived in the village of Ahuelican. He rode a fine black stallion. Of all the young men, he was the handsomest, and the best horseman, and he knew it very well. When the girls smiled at Canciano, he didn't smile back. He was too proud, and he didn't think he needed to smile. Why should he? He was the best.

One day a cheerful young man came riding from Mexico City to the village of Ahuelican. His name was Rafael, and he was so good-natured that people liked to be with him. He made them laugh. Rafael was tired of city life. He preferred the country. He rode a short, rough-coated horse he called Amigo. Amigo had been running wild in the hills with a herd when Rafael caught him and gentled him. Rafael loved Amigo even though the horse had short legs and looked rough. Rafael had short legs and looked rather rough himself, but he made people laugh at his jokes. He always laughed with them, and his white teeth flashed in his brown face.

All the girls liked Rafael. He made them feel happy.

Canciano was jealous. When Rafael spoke to him politely, Canciano turned away and would not answer. His heart was full of anger. Why did everyone like Rafael so much? Couldn't they see that Canciano himself was the best?

Canciano decided that he would make Rafael look foolish. He would challenge him to a race. Then everyone would see how rough and ordinary Rafael and his horse were. They would see how handsome Canciano was on his fine, black, long-legged stallion. They would see how well he sat his horse and how well his horse ran. They would know he was the best.

Canciano looked stern when he challenged Rafael. "Do you dare race me on your horse? We can invite the whole village."

Rafael smiled good-naturedly. "Sure. I'll race you," he said.

It seemed to Canciano that Rafael didn't take the race seriously. That made him angrier than ever. He galloped away frowning.

The morning of the race, Rafael looked happy and confident. But Canciano was angry and nervous. He spoke to his beautiful black horse in a harsh voice. His legs were tense on the horse's sides, and he held the reins tightly. The horse felt his rider's anger. It made him feel nervous and confused.

Rafael sat lightly on Amigo. He stroked him and spoke softly as he waited for the race to begin. "We can do it, Amigo."

When the race began, he held the reins loosely and clicked his tongue to make Amigo go. Rafael had watched the wild herd and had chosen Amigo carefully. He had short legs, but he was fast and strong.

Rafael's kind voice encouraged Amigo. He ran like the wind.

Rafael and Amigo won the race. Everyone was happy that good-natured Rafael had won.

Canciano's heart burned. Rafael saw his angry face, and he felt sure Canciano would try to harm him and get revenge. Perhaps Canciano would steal Amigo. Or he might lay a trap for Rafael. Or he might try to turn people against him. But the more Rafael thought about it, the more sure he was that Canciano would try to find a nahual to harm him.

Just as Rafael expected, Canciano was determined to get revenge. He wanted to kill Rafael, but Rafael was so strong and quick that Canciano knew he could never beat him in a fight. So sure enough, Canciano hired a nahual named Luis to kill Rafael.

"I'll pay you when he's dead," Canciano told Luis. "I'll give you my black stallion." Canciano didn't love his beautiful horse. He was glad to trade him for revenge.

Luis-the-nahual didn't know Rafael well, and he didn't care about him. He just wanted the beautiful horse.

"All I have to do is find him asleep," he told Canciano. "Then I can eat his heart."

But Rafael was smart and took precautions. He knew that the nahual could harm him only when he was asleep, so for seven days, he ate garlic in the morning and fasted all the rest of the day, eating only a little food at night. Eating garlic and fasting made it possible for him to stay awake.

Luis-the-nahual had to turn himself into an owl so he could watch Rafael and eat his heart. It wasn't so easy to change into an owl. After dark, he had to leap into the air and turn a flip. Only a strong, lively person could leap high into the air and flip like that, but Luis could do it, and he did. He turned into an owl. He would be an owl until sunrise. Luis-the-nahual-owl perched in a tree outside Rafael's house.

Rafael was sitting on the porch. He sat there all night, resting in his chair. But he didn't sleep.

Luis-the-nahual-owl watched and waited all night. When dawn came and he became a man again, he was frustrated. But he flipped and turned into an owl again the next night. And the next night. And the next. Every night, he flipped, changed, and waited. But smart Rafael kept eating garlic and fasting. He didn't go to sleep.

On the seventh day at sunrise when Luis-the-nahual turned back into a person, he was so tired and so frustrated, he shouted to Rafael: "I've been trying to eat your heart for a week. Why don't you ever sleep?"

"You can flip twenty times, but you'll never eat my heart,"

Rafael answered. But he spoke softly and smiled his good-natured smile.

Luis couldn't help himself; he had to smile back. "Okay, you win. Never mind about eating your heart. Let's go eat breakfast."

So Rafael and Luis went off together to have breakfast. On the road, they saw Canciano and waved. He frowned and shook his fist at Luis, but Luis didn't notice. Rafael had just told a joke, and they were laughing.

LALITO AND THE NAHUAL

Every culture has stories of a smart child outwitting a not-so-nice adult. The Mesoamericans are no different. Here is a contemporary story from Ahuelican, Guerrero, Mexico, collected by Lalo Julian.

Lalito was a bright little boy who lived in the village of Ahuelican. He noticed that there was something odd about his teacher, Señor Vargas, and he was determined to find out what it was. The other students didn't seem to notice, but sometimes when Lalito looked at Señor Vargas, he thought he could see a bit of fur on his neck. Other times it seemed that some little feathers were growing in his hair. Once when Lalito looked out of the corner of his eye, Señor Vargas's hand looked like a claw. And often when the class was quiet and Señor Vargas was reading at his desk, his face looked like a jaguar face. Lalito believed that Señor Vargas was a nahual.

Lalito didn't say a word to anyone about Señor Vargas, but he watched him carefully. He noticed that when everyone, including Señor Vargas, was reading quietly, he wasn't reading a school book. Instead he read from a big book that looked very old and didn't have any words on the cover. Lalito also noticed that if anyone went to Señor Vargas's desk to ask a question, he would close his book and quickly put it inside his desk. Lalito believed the book held important secrets.

Lalito watched and waited for his chance, but Señor Vargas never left his desk for long, so Lalito decided that he must come back to the school when no one was around. It was a tiny schoolhouse, and because the door couldn't be locked very well, it would be easy to get into. The problem was finding a time when no one would notice him. It must be daytime, because someone would notice a light at night.

Lalito decided that he would hide in the small closet where the broom and a few books were kept. He planned to slip into the closet when no one was watching and stay after school. When everyone was gone, he could read Señor Vargas's book.

On one beautiful spring day when the class went out for after-noon recess, Señor Vargas went outside also and took a turn around the school yard. Lalito seized his chance and slipped into the closet. He left the door open just a crack so he could peek out.

When everyone came back in, Señor Vargas didn't even miss Lalito. He just hurried through the last lesson and dismissed school. All the students were eager to go out into the beautiful spring weather, but Señor Vargas stayed behind. He watched out the window until he was sure all the students were gone. Then he hurried to his desk and took out the book.

He read one page carefully, then leaped high, flipped in the air, turned into a shiny black horse, and trotted out the door. Señor Vargas really was a nahual!

Lalito ran to the window. He saw the horse leap high into the air and flip. The horse disappeared, and Señor Vargas came walking back toward the school.

Lalito dashed to the closet.

He watched Señor Vargas jump, flip, and turn into a bull, and then leap, flip again, and turn into a great turtle. As a turtle, he seemed to have a hard time leaping high enough to do a good flip. When he finally turned back into himself, he seemed tired and went home.

As soon as Lalito was sure that Señor Vargas was really gone, he ran to his desk. He was so excited that his hands shook as he lifted the book out of the drawer. He read until it grew dark. As he walked home, his heart drummed in his chest. He believed he could learn to change just as Señor Vargas had done.

Every day Lalito studied how to become a nahual. Some days he hid in the closet as he had done before; some days he went home and came back to the school later. He read the whole book, and one day he decided he was ready to begin changing. But before he could begin, the schoolhouse door flew open, and in walked Señor Vargas. He saw Lalito, and he was furious. Lalito could tell by the expression on his face that he was dangerous.

Lalito needed to get away. Ready or not, he had to change.

He leaped into the air, flipped, and turned into a young jack-rabbit, hardly more than a bunny. But Señor Vargas leaped, flipped, and turned into a coyote. It chased the young jackrabbit around the room. Lalito knew he was about to be caught. Even a very young jackrabbit has strong legs. He leaped, flipped in the air, and turned into a deer. It was quite a young deer, only a fawn, but even a fawn can outrun a coyote.

The deer jumped over desks and chairs and ran toward the door, but the coyote leaped, flipped, and turned into a jaguar. A jaguar is fast and fierce. Its strong jaws could crush a young deer's head in a moment. But deer are great jumpers. The young deer leaped high into the air, flipped, and turned into a hummingbird.

Hummingbirds are tiny, but they are fast and can fly high. It flew up near the ceiling; its small wings were only a whir in the air. Before the hummingbird could reach the open window, the jaguar leaped, flipped, and turned into a hawk. The hawk flew after the hummingbird. Even a hummingbird cannot go faster than a hawk, and the hawk could eat him in one bite. Lalito had to think fast. All the creatures he turned into were small and young. How could he escape?

Lalito knew that hawks ate only meat. He concentrated hard. The hummingbird easily flipped in the air, and a shower of sesame seeds fell on the floor. Even though there were a lot of seeds, they were tiny, and Lalito felt cramped.

The hawk flipped in the air and turned into a rooster. The rooster began greedily eating the sesame seeds. It ate all the seeds that were scattered around the schoolroom except for one little seed that had fallen into a crack in the floor.

Sesame seeds are not good jumpers. Just the same, cramped as he was, Lalito gathered his strength, concentrated hard, flew into the air, flipped, and turned into a puppy. The puppy pounced, and that was the end of the rooster.

Now Lalito is the only nahual in Ahuelican.

THE DEVIL'S CAVE

A contemporary story from Ahuelican, Guerrero, Mexico, blends magic, mystery, and horror.

Feliciano was a poor man. He was the poorest man in Ahuelican, but he seemed just as happy as his name would suggest. He worked just enough to keep himself in beans and squash, and the rest of the time he sat on the porch of his little hut and watched the days go by.

"You are too poor," Homero told him. "Why don't you do something to make some money? You barely have enough to eat, and you have only one old shirt."

Feliciano shook his head and smiled his contented smile.

"I don't understand you," Homero said. "How can you be so happy?"

Feliciano answered politely. "My friend, I could have more money than anyone in the village. I could be the richest man in the state of Guerrero, even in all of Mexico, but that is not my choice. I'll tell you why."

He pointed to a mountain just over the way. "That's where the riches are. They are in the devil's cave. I've been there twice, but I'll never go there again.

"It was during Semana Santa. My friend Julio and I knew that in the week of Semana Santa the devil is not at home in his cave, and a person can enter it from an opening in the mountain. The devil's cave is full of gold, jewels, fine horses, beautiful women, and all kinds of treasures. Julio and I wanted to get our hands on the gold.

"My old uncle, who is dead now, told us where to find the cave, and he gave us good advice. 'Think only of the gold and keep your eyes straight ahead. You must not be distracted for even a moment or the devil will drink your blood. Just get the gold and run out at once.'

"When we got in the cave, it was just as my old uncle had said. I tried not to look at all the dazzling things around me—colorful feather art, splendid cloth, precious jewels, noble horses, and beautiful women. I couldn't help seeing them, but I tried not to pay them the least attention. I only had eyes for the gold. I could see it deep inside the cave, and I kept walking toward it.

"Julio was smoking a cigarette. He stopped to look at a horse. It was such a fine horse, he forgot the gold, and mounted. I could see it all from the corner of my eye. I didn't want to see even that much. I didn't want the devil to drink my blood. I turned and ran from the cave. Julio did not follow.

"I knew that I would have to wait a year to bring my friend out of the cave. When the year finished and it was Semana Santa

again, I returned to the devil's cave. I was afraid, but I went in. I wanted to save Julio.

"Inside, things were just as before. I didn't let the beautiful things, not even the gorgeous women who came up to me, take my attention. But I saw Julio mounted on the wonderful horse, a cigarette in his fingers, just as he had been when I left him.

"I helped him from the horse and led him outside. He moved slowly, but we went to his house. He saw his wife and children. Then he died. He was perfectly white—no color at all. The devil had drunk his blood.

"I know how to get the gold, but I don't have an appetite for it any more. I'd rather be poor."

THE POSSUM'S TALE

Stories of wicked old women and tricksters are familiar to us all. Perhaps this one derives from European stories told by the priests. Perhaps the Mesoamericans had their own trickster tales, as did the Native Americans in what is now the United States.

A long time ago before people had fire, a smart, brave old woman noticed something bright fall from a comet. She thought because it was bright it might be good, and she wanted it, so she ran and snatched some of the fire before it burned out. She took it home and took good care of it. She made a hearth, and she fed the fire. She never let it go out.

The smart, brave old woman was selfish. She learned to cook with the fire, and she kept herself warm with it. She never shared with anybody, but the people could smell her good food, and when they walked by her house, they could feel that it was warm even in the coldest weather.

The people thought that it was wrong of the old woman to keep the fire just for herself. They thought that all the people needed fire. So they went to the old woman's house and politely asked for some of her fire. "Grandmother, please share your fire with us. Let us carry a little to our homes."

But the old woman was not only selfish, she was ferocious. She brandished a torch and drove all the people away from her door.

The old woman wasn't the only smart one around. Possum was just as shrewd as she was. When he learned that the old woman had managed to keep fire but would not share it, he went to the people.

"You want fire," he said. "I can get you fire, and I'll do it, but only if you promise never to eat me."

Everyone laughed. "You little old thing!" they said. "You are no match for that old woman!"

They kept laughing.

"Stop making fun of me!" Possum said. "I'll show you a trick or two. This very evening, you'll see what I can do."

That evening he went from house to house and told all the people that he was about to get fire from the old woman, and he would bring them some. Then he went to the old woman's house.

When he arrived he said, "Good evening, Grandmother. This cold is killing me. May I stand by your fire for a little while?"

The old woman didn't think there was any harm in such a little creature, so she let him stand by her fire.

Possum crept closer and closer. He held up his tail and stood right against the fire. Then he put his tail down. It caught on fire. It blazed up.

Possum ran out of the old woman's house, his tail blazing. He dashed to all the other houses and shared the fire with all the people.

The hair never grew back on Possum's tail. Even today, possums have bald tails and people have fire.

CHIOCONEJO RABBIT AND COYOTE

In the Mesoamerican trickster tales, the coyote is out-smarted by the rabbit. This is a contemporary Aztec tale that suggests an outside, perhaps European, influence.

Coyote wanted to eat Chioconejo Rabbit, and he tried to catch him many times, but Chioconejo Rabbit was clever. He always managed to trick Coyote. Once when he saw Coyote coming his way, he ran to a hollow place in the mountain and put up his arms as if he were holding up the mountain. Then he called, "Coyote, come help me!"

Coyote came close. "What are you doing with your arms up like that?"

"Oh, Coyote, I am holding up the mountain. If I let go, it will fall and everything will be destroyed. Help me!"

"You are doing okay. Why should I help?"

"Because my arms are so tired, I can't hold up the mountain much longer. You take it for a little while so I can get a drink and rest my arms. I'll give you all my black chickens if you help me. They are the most delicious chickens of all. You can see them there across the field."

Coyote loved to eat chicken. He looked across the field and saw a flock of black birds. He thought, I have never eaten black chicken. Maybe it really is the most delicious chicken of all.

"Okay," he told Chioconejo Rabbit. "Go get a drink. I'll hold the mountain for a little while."

When he put up his arms to hold the mountain, Chioconejo Rabbit hopped away.

Coyote waited a long time for Chioconejo Rabbit to come back. He got terribly tired. Finally he got so tired, he couldn't hold his arms up any more.

I have to let go of the mountain, he thought. But he was afraid the mountain would fall and crush him. He counted, "One, two, three." Then he turned loose and ran.

Nothing happened.

Chioconejo Rabbit has tricked me, Coyote thought. I'm going to get even—I'll eat his delicious black chickens, and then I'll eat him.

He ran across the field toward the flock of birds. But they flew into the air.

"What is this? Chickens can't fly like that!"

Then Coyote saw that the birds weren't chickens at all. They were buzzards. He would never eat a stinky, tough buzzard even if he could catch one.

So he went on his hungry way, grumbling about Chioconejo Rabbit.

OTHER TELLINGS

Bernardino Sahagún's *Florentine Codex, General History of the Things of New Spain,* is the first and best source of information about the Aztecs. It was written in the first half of the sixteenth century. Sahagún arrived in Mexico eight years after the Conquest and did extensive, thorough research with the indigenous people. Because of fear that his work would encourage paganism, it was suppressed and was actually lost for three hundred years until a man named Muñoz found it in the convent of Tolosi in Navarre. The next important work is Father Juan de Torquemada's *Monarchia Indiana* (Indian Monarchies), published in Seville in 1615. He drew from the Codex and included observations on the native people's religion.

Other recorders of the mythology followed. The early tellings are largely fragmentary. This book has been drawn primarily from secondary sources and retold and developed in ways to make it accessible for contemporary readers while retaining as much of the original flavor as possible. I am not a scholar of Nahuatl or anthropology, but a storyteller who has relied on contemporary Nahuatl speakers for the style and pacing of the stories. (See Lewis Spence, *The Myths of Mexico and Peru,* pp. 56–58, for a description of the earliest works and their sequence.)

Birth of the Fifth Sun

"The Aztec Sun." Middlesex, England: Hamlyn, 1986. http://
www.storymall.com/aztecsun/aztec.htm (accessed November 24, 2006).

Bierhorst, John, ed. "The Fifth Sun." In *The Hungry Woman: Myths
and Legends of the Aztecs*. New York: William Morrow, 1984, pp.
34–35.

Bierhorst, John. *The Mythology of Mexico and Central America*. New
York: William Morrow, 1990, p. 182.

Doyle, Diana. "Narrative." *Aztec and Mayan Mythology*. Yale-New
Haven Teachers Institute. http://www.yale.edu/ynhti/cur-
riculum/units/1994/3/94.03.04.x.html (accessed November 24, 2006).

Markman, Roberta H., and Peter T. Markman. *The Flayed God: The
Mythology of Mesoamerica*. New York: HarperCollins, 1992, pp.
120–125.

Nicholson, Irene. *Mexican and Central American Mythology*. London:
Hamlyn, 1967, pp. 54, 72–73.

Taube, Karl. *Aztec and Maya Myths*. Austin: University of Texas
Press, 1993, pp. 41–44.

"Legend of the Fifth Sun." *Aztec Folk Tales*. San Diego, Calif.: San
Diego County Office of Education, 1997. http://www.
sdcoe.k12.ca.us/score/aztec/fifthsun.html (accessed November 24, 2006).

"Origin of the Gods and the World." *Aztec Legends, Stories
and Myths*. http://www.geocities.com/Athens/Acade-

my/3088/legends.html (accessed November 24, 2006).

"The Sun and Moon Story." *Aztec Gods and Goddesses.* http://library.thinkquest.org/27981/god.html (accessed November 24, 2006).

The Buzzard Husband

Bierhorst, John. *The Mythology of Mexico and Central America.* New York: William Morrow, 1990, pp. 120–123.

Giddings, Ruth Warner. "The Man Who Became a Buzzard." *Yaqui Myths and Legends,* 1959 (copyright not registered or renewed). http://www.sacred-texts.com/nam/sw/yml/yml20.htm (accessed November 24, 2006).

Orellana, Sandra L. "Folk Literature of the Tzutujil Maya." *Anthropos* 70 (1975): 839–876. (The phrases "dead horses, dead cows, dead dogs, dead chickens, and dead pigs. Buzzards only eat dead things" and "Horrible buzzard!" are direct quotations from the original tale as reported by Orellana. Similarly, Taggart's version includes, "Horrible, filthy animal.")

Taggart, James. M. *Nahuat Myth and Social Structure.* Austin: University of Texas Press, 1983, pp. 208–209 ("The Lazy Husband," two variants). (There are other stories in which the buzzard lives for some time in the form of a human. One example is "The Vulture," by Alberto Pablo Ravírez and collected by Ronald J. Anderson, Texas A&M International University. http://www.tamiu.edu/~randerson/ [accessed November 24, 2006]. Another is "The Hunter and the

Buzzard." First People, Native American Legends. http://
www.firstpeople.us/FP-Html-Legends/TheHunterAndThe-
Buzzard-Cherokee.html [accessed November 24, 2006].)

Chioconejo Rabbit and Coyote

Contemporary story from Ahuelican, Guerrero, as reported by
Lalo Julian.

One variant of this story is recorded in Giddings, Ruth Warner, "Rabbit and Coyote," *Yaqui Myths and Legends*, 1959
(copyright not registered or renewed). http://www.
sacred-texts.com/nam/sw/yml/yml20.htm (accessed November 24, 2006).

Corn Mountain

"Attributes." Quetzalcoatl. Wikipedia. http://en.wikipedia.
org/wiki/Quetzalcoatl (accessed November 24, 2006).

Bierhorst, John, ed. "True Corn." In *The Hungry Woman: Myths and
Legends of the Aztecs*. New York: William Morrow, 1984, pp.
32–33.

Bierhorst, John. *The Mythology of Mexico and Central America*. New
York: William Morrow, 1990, pp. 86, 147.

Markman, Roberta H., and Peter T. Markman. *The Flayed God: The
Mythology of Mesoamerica*. New York: HarperCollins, 1992, pp.
134–135, 182–183.

Vigil, Angel. *The Eagle on the Cactus: Traditional Stories from Mexico*.
Englewood, Colo.: Libraries Unlimited, 2000, pp. 54–55.

Read, Kay Almere, and Jason J. Gonzalez. *Handbook of Mesoamerican Mythology.* Santa Barbara, Calif.: ABC-CLIO, 2000, p. 225.

Taube, Karl. *Aztec and Maya Myths.* Austin: University of Texas Press, 1993.

The Devil's Cave

Contemporary story from Ahuelican, Guerrero, Mexico, as reported by Lalo Julian.

Five Suns

"The Aztec Sun." Middlesex, England: Hamlyn, 1986. http://www.storymall.com/aztecsun/aztec.htm (accessed November 24, 2006).

Bierhorst, John, ed. "The First Sun." In *The Hungry Woman: Myths and Legends of the Aztecs.* New York: William Morrow, pp. 25–27.

Bierhorst, John, ed. "Monkeys, Turkeys, and Fish." In *The Hungry Woman: Myths and Legends of the Aztecs.* New York: William Morrow, 1984, pp. 27–28.

Caso, Alfonso. *The Aztecs: People of the Sun.* Norman: University of Oklahoma Press, 1958, pp. 14–20.

Kirkpatrick, Berni. "The Creation and the Legend of the Four Suns." *Myths and Legends, Aztec Mythology.* http://www.create.org/myth/997myth.htm (accessed November 24, 2006).

Roy, Cal. *The Serpent and the Sun: Myths of the Mexican World.* New York: Farrar, Straus and Giroux, 1972, pp. 21–29.

Lalito and the Nahual

Contemporary story from Ahuelican, Guerrero, as reported by Lalo Julian.

Master Log

Bierhorst, John, ed. "Master Log." In *The Hungry Woman: Myths and Legends of the Aztecs*. New York: William Morrow, 1984, pp. 52–55.

Mackenzie, Donald A. *Myths of Pre-Columbian America*. London: Gresham, 1924, p. 283.

Markman, Roberta H., and Peter T. Markman. *The Flayed God: The Mythology of Mesoamerica*. New York: HarperCollins, 1992, pp. 361–362.

Nicholson, Irene. *Mexican and Central American Mythology*. London: Hamlyn, 1967, pp. 99–102.

Read, Kay Almere, and Jason J. Gonzalez. *Handbook of Mesoamerican Mythology*. Santa Barbara, Calif.: ABC-CLIO, 2000, p. 226.

Sahagún, Bernardino. *Florentine Codex, General History of the Things of New Spain*. Books 4 and 5, "The Soothsayers" and "The Omens." Translated from the Nahuatl with notes by Arthur J. O. Anderson and Charles E. Dibble. Salt Lake City: University of Utah Press, 1957, pp. 25–26.

Spence, Lewis. *The Myths of Mexico and Peru*. Boston: Longwood Press, 1977, pp. 63–64.

Music Is Born

Nicholson, Irene. *Mexican and Central American Mythology*. London: Hamlyn, 1967, p. 31.

Bierhorst, John. *The Mythology of Mexico and Central America*. New York: William Morrow, 1990, p. 147.

The Pepper Man

Bierhorst, John, ed. "The King's Daughter and the Pepper Man." In *The Hungry Woman: Myths and Legends of the Aztecs*. New York: William Morrow, 1984, pp. 45–50.

Dils, Lorna. "Tezcatlipoca and the King of Tula." *Aztec Mythology*. Yale-New Haven Teachers Institute. http://www.yale.edu/ynhti/curriculum/units/1994/3/94.03.03.x.html (accessed November 20, 2006).

Mackenzie, Donald A. *Myths of Pre-Columbian America*. London: Gresham, 1924, p. 282.

Markman, Roberta H., and Peter T. Markman. *The Flayed God: The Mythology of Mesoamerica*. New York: HarperCollins, 1992, pp. 356–357.

Nicholson, Irene. *Mexican and Central American Mythology*. London: Hamlyn, 1967, pp. 98–99.

Roy, Cal. *The Serpent and the Sun: Myths of the Mexican World*. New York: Farrar, Straus and Giroux, 1972.

Sahagún, Bernardino. *Florentine Codex, General History of the Things of New Spain*. Books 4 and 5, "The Soothsayers" and "The Omens." Translated from the Nahuatl with notes by Arthur

J. O. Anderson and Charles E. Dibble. Salt Lake City: University of Utah Press, 1957, pp. 17–18.

Spence, Lewis. *The Myths of Mexico and Peru*. Boston: Longwood Press, 1977, pp. 61–63.

The Possum's Tale

Bierhorst, John. *The Mythology of Mexico and Central America*. New York: William Morrow, 1990, pp. 77–78, 120–123.

Vigil, Angel. *The Eagle on the Cactus: Traditional Stories from Mexico*. Englewood, Colo.: Libraries Unlimited, 2000, pp. 70–71.

Quetzalcoatl Falls

Baldwin, Neil. *Legends of the Plumed Serpent: Biography of a Mexican God*. New York: PublicAffairs, 1998, p. 9.

Bierhorst, John, ed. "The Flight of Quetzalcoatl." In *The Hungry Woman: Myths and Legends of the Aztecs*. New York: William Morrow, 1984, pp. 55–61.

Mackenzie, Donald A. *Myths of Pre-Columbian America*. London: Gresham, 1924. p. 282.

Markman, Roberta H., and Peter T. Markman. *The Flayed God: The Mythology of Mesoamerica*. New York: HarperCollins, 1992, pp. 371–377.

Nicholson, Irene. *Mexican and Central American Mythology*. London: Hamlyn, 1967, p. 88.

Roy, Cal. *The Serpent and the Sun: Myths of the Mexican World*. New York: Farrar, Straus and Giroux, 1972, pp. 47–58.

Sahagún, Bernardino. *Florentine Codex, General History of the Things of New Spain*. Books 4 and 5, "The Soothsayers" and "The Omens." Translated from the Nahuatl with notes by Arthur J. O. Anderson and Charles E. Dibble. Salt Lake City: University of Utah Press, 1957, pp. 15–16.

Spence, Lewis. *The Myths of Mexico and Peru*. Boston: Longwood Press, 1977, pp. 60–61.

Rafael Outsmarts the Nahual

Contemporary story from Ahuelican, Guerrero, Mexico, as reported by Lalo Julian.

For a discussion of contemporary belief in *nahuals*, see Horcasitas, Fernando, *The Aztecs Then and Now*, Mexico City: Editorial Minutiae Mexicana, 1992, pp. 118–119.

Tata and Nena

Nicholson, Irene. *Mexican and Central American Mythology*. London: Hamlyn, 1967, pp. 53–54.

Read, Kay Almere, and Jason J. Gonzalez. *Handbook of Mesoamerican Mythology*. Santa Barbara, Calif.: ABC-CLIO, 2000, p. 251.

Taube, Karl. *Aztec and Maya Myths*. Austin: University of Texas Press, 1993, p. 36.

"Tata and Nena." *Metareligion*. http://www.meta-religion.com/World_Religions/Ancient_religions/ (accessed November 24, 2006).

Tezca's Music

Mackenzie, Donald A. *Myths of Pre-Columbian America*. London: Gresham, 1924, pp. 278–279.

Nicholson, Irene. *Mexican and Central American Mythology*. London: Hamlyn, 1967, p. 31.

Roy, Cal. *The Serpent and the Sun: Myths of the Mexican World*. New York: Farrar, Straus and Giroux, 1972, pp. 47–58.

Sahagún, Bernardino. *Florentine Codex, General History of the Things of New Spain*. Books 4 and 5, "The Soothsayers" and "The Omens." Translated from the Nahuatl with notes by Arthur J. O. Anderson and Charles E. Dibble. Salt Lake City: University of Utah Press, 1957, pp. 21–22.

Tezca Shows His Power

Sahagún, Bernardino. *Florentine Codex, General History of the Things of New Spain*. Books 4 and 5, "The Soothsayers" and "The Omens." Translated from the Nahuatl with notes by Arthur J. O. Anderson and Charles E. Dibble. Salt Lake City: University of Utah Press, 1957, pp. 23, 27. (Various magical acts of power are mentioned in numerous sources. This story is the most authentic, but I have relied on memory and imagination to write this transitional tale to unify the work.)

The Thunder Spirits' New Cook

Bierhorst, John, ed. *The Mythology of Mexico and Central America*. New York: William Morrow, 1990, pp. 116–117.

Taggart, James M. *Nahuat Myth and Social Structure*. Austin: University of Texas Press, 1983, pp. 223–224 (includes a variant called "The Hunter").

Who Can Teach the People?

Bierhorst, John, ed. "Quetzalcoatl in Tula." In *The Hungry Woman: Myths and Legends of the Aztecs*. New York: William Morrow, 1984, pp. 38–41.

Bierhorst, John. *The Mythology of Mexico and Central America*. New York: William Morrow, 1990, p. 159.

Nicholson, Irene. *Mexican and Central American Mythology*. London: Hamlyn, 1967, p. 87.

Quetzalcoatl, The Man, The Myth, The Legend. http://groups.msn.com/AncientWisdomNewMillenium/quetzalcoatl2.msnw. (accessed November 20, 2006).

Sahagún, Bernardino. *Florentine Codex, General History of the Things of New Spain*. Books 4 and 5, "The Soothsayers" and "The Omens." Translated from the Nahuatl with notes by Arthur J. O. Anderson and Charles E. Dibble. Salt Lake City, Utah: University of Utah Press, 1957, p. 13, 13f.

Who Will Be the People?

Baldwin, Neil. *Legends of the Plumed Serpent: Biography of a Mexican God*. New York: PublicAffairs, 1998, pp. 8–9.

Bierhorst, John, ed. "Up from the Dead Land." In *The Hungry Woman: Myths and Legends of the Aztecs*. New York: William Morrow, 1984, pp. 29–32.

Bierhorst, John. *The Mythology of Mexico and Central America.* New York: William Morrow, 1990, pp. 183–184.

Caso, Alfonso. *The Aztecs: People of the Sun.* Norman: University of Oklahoma Press, 1958, p. 24.

Markman, Roberta H., and Peter T. Markman. *The Flayed God: The Mythology of Mesoamerica.* New York: Harper Collins, 1992, pp. 134–135.

Nicholson, Irene. *Mexican and Central American Mythology.* London: Hamlyn, 1967, p. 27.

Read, Kay Almere, and Jason J. Gonzalez. *Handbook of Mesoamerican Mythology.* Santa Barbara, Calif.: ABC-CLIO, 2000, p. 224.

Taube, Karl. *Aztec and Maya Myths.* Austin: University of Texas Press, 1993, pp. 37–39.

Vigil, Angel. *The Eagle on the Cactus: Traditional Stories from Mexico.* Englewood, Colo.: Libraries Unlimited, 2000, pp. 52–53.

SOURCES

Baldwin, Neil. *Legends of the Plumed Serpent: Biography of a Mexican God*. New York: PublicAffairs, 1998.

Beals, Carlton. *Stories Told by the Aztecs Before the Spaniards Came*. London: Abelard-Schuman, 1970.

Bierhorst, John. *History and Mythology of the Aztecs: The Codex Chimalpopoca*. Tucson: University of Arizona Press, 1992.

Bierhorst, John. *The Mythology of Mexico and Central America*. New York: William Morrow, 1990.

Bierhorst, John, ed. *The Hungry Woman: Myths and Legends of the Aztecs*. New York: William Morrow, 1984.

Burland, C. A., and Werner Forman. *Feathered Serpent and Smoking Mirror*. New York: Putnam, 1975.

Caso, Alfonso. *The Aztecs: People of the Sun*. Norman: University of Oklahoma Press, 1958.

Díaz, Gisele, and Alan Rodgers. *The Codex Borgia: A Full-Color Restoration of the Ancient Mexican Manuscript*. New York: Dover Publications, 1993.

Horcasitas, Fernando. *The Aztecs Then and Now*. Mexico City: Editorial Minutiae Mexicana, 1992.

Mackenzie, Donald A. *Myths of Pre-Columbian America*. London: Gresham, 1924.

Markman, Roberta H., and Peter T. Markman. *The Flayed God: The Mythology of Mesoamerica*. New York: HarperCollins, 1992.

Nicholson, Irene. *Mexican and Central American Mythology*. London: Hamlyn, 1967.

Orellana, Sandra L. "Folk Literature of the Tzutujil Maya." *Anthropos* 70 (1975): 839–876.

Pasztory, Esther. *Aztec Art*. Norman: University of Oklahoma Press, 1983.

Read, Kay Almere, and Jason J. Gonzalez. *Handbook of Mesoamerican Mythology*. Santa Barbara, Calif.: ABC-CLIO, 2000.

Ross, Kurt, commentary. *Codex Mendoza: Aztec Manuscript*. n.p.: Miller Graphics, Productions Liber S.A., C-H Fribourg, 1978.

Roy, Cal. *The Serpent and the Sun: Myths of the Mexican World*. New York: Farrar, Straus and Giroux, 1972.

Sahagún, Bernardino. *Florentine Codex, General History of the Things of New Spain*. Books 4 and 5, "The Soothsayers" and "The Omens." Translated from the Nahuatl with notes by Arthur J. O. Anderson and Charles E. Dibble. Salt Lake City University of Utah Press, 1957.

Spence, Lewis. *The Myths of Mexico and Peru*. Boston: Longwood Press, 1977.

Taggart, James M. *Nahuat Myth and Social Structure*. Austin: University of Texas Press, 1983.

Taube, Karl. *Aztec and Maya Myths*. Austin: University of Texas Press, 1993.

Vigil, Angel. *The Eagle on the Cactus: Traditional Stories from Mexico.* Englewood, Colo.: Libraries Unlimited, 2000.

JO HARPER is also the author of the award-winning young-adult novels *Delfino's Journey* and *Teresa's Journey* (both from TTUP), as well as many works for younger readers, including *Jalapeño Hal, Prairie Dog Pioneers, Finding Daddy, Mexicatl,* and *I Could Eat You Up!* She lives in Houston.